for Neel,
my best friend

FADE IN:

EXT. HOUSE – DAY

Anna and her family sit on the front porch.
Sunflowers bloom beneath the windowsills.
The sky is clear. It's a perfect spring day.

> DAD
> Isn't it lovely here?

SISTER twists a flower stem between her
fingers.

> SISTER
> I'm glad I never left.

MOM leans back in her wicker chair.

> MOM
> Wouldn't it be great
> if this was real?

> ANNA
> (Sighs)
> Wouldn't it?

CUT TO:

The real world.

ACT ONE

POV

All I can see
is the front lawn
from the tiny window
in the basement.

It's only
mid September
and already
the grass has
lost its color.

It died before
fall had a chance
to begin.

It died like
we somehow
skipped from
summer to winter

and I just
didn't notice
the sky getting
darker.

4

MAGICIAN

Today,
Samantha
is coming home

for the first time
in three years.

My sister is
a magician.

(Well, not really.)

But she *has*
perfected her
vanishing act.

One day,
she was here.

And then,
she disappeared.

She left
no promises
to come back
and visit.

All she left
were my
text messages
on *read.*

But last week
she called Dad

and asked
if she could
finally
move back.

HOMETOWN

I live in Garey,
Pennsylvania.

Where the sky
hangs like a
gray curtain
over acres
and acres of
nothingness.

It's a town you
drive in and
out of—
a pit stop on
the way to
Philadelphia.

I swear, once
you enter,
it's like
everything
is tinted in
the dullest filter.

My sister
had seen things
differently:

*Your lens
needs adjusting.*

This place
can be beautiful.

Said the girl
who left.

ABOVE ME

I can hear Mom
upstairs, in the kitchen.

She's been rushing
to make Samantha's
favorite dinner:

brisket with
onions and carrots.

No one makes
brisket like my mom.
(That is, according to
my mom.)

This morning I saw
she was wearing
a pink sundress with
her hair pulled up.

Even though
there's frost outside
and the forecast says
to expect heavy rain.

All she said was,
It's a special day.

As if that somehow
changes the weather.

CORRECTION:

Brisket *was*
my sister's favorite,
before, when we
used to know her.

Before she
turned 18
and jumped into
the passenger seat
of her boyfriend's
Mercedes.

Before they
drove up east,
toward New York—
or who knows?

Maybe they drove
past Manhattan,
all the way up
to New England.

Maybe they took
a wrong turn
and got lost in Maine,
in the cedar trees.

Maybe that's why
she hasn't been calling.

SISTERS

Samantha and I
used to share
the second bedroom
upstairs.

We would share
so many things:

Movie nights.
Snowball fights.
Hot chocolates.

We even had
the same hair:
thick, brown curls.

She'd let me
try her makeup on.
Even the
fake eyelashes.
*(Just don't
tell Mom!)*

Things changed
when she started
her junior year,
started going out
more often.

Started calling me
*my annoying
little sister*
when her boyfriend
came over.

The distance
between us grew.
Then she left.

Now, we're
miles apart.

SETTING
THE SCENE

When she moved,
I moved, too.
Below ground,
to the basement.

I live in the basement,
but the basement is
my basement,
and I love it.

I am the
only one who
walks down the
creaky stairs onto
the peeling carpet.

I am the
only one who
squashes spiders
that creep through the
cracked walls.

I have a desk,
a bed, a couch,
and a dresser.

And of course,
I have my TV.
That's all I
really need.

13

I WATCH MOVIES

Comedy, romance,
fantasy, mystery.

I watch the old
Hollywood movies in
black and white.

I watch the new
action movies
with the best CGI
money can buy.

I've watched all the
teen comedies
my parents
grew up with.

(I've seen
John Bender
thrust his fist
in the air
at the end of
The Breakfast Club
a dozen times.)

I've seen all
the musicals
my sister used to play

the soundtracks to
in the living room.
Rent, Hairspray,
and *Mamma Mia!*

There are only
a few films
I don't watch:

Scary movies
make me anxious.

And I don't like
sad movies either.

Who wants to
cry on purpose?

EXTRA

I sneak upstairs,
hoping my parents
won't notice me
grabbing a bag of
chips before dinner.

But they usually
don't notice me.

Like an extra on a film set,
I fade in and out
of the background:

more like the scenery
and less like an actor.

GETTING READY

Mom sprays Febreze
to hide the smell of
her cigarette smoke

while Dad vacuums
the same corner of
dirt brown carpet

over and
over and
over.

I want to tell him,
*Some stains just
won't come out.*

Dad catches my eye
before I can sneak
back downstairs.

He looks like he also
wants to say something,
but doesn't.

MY DAD

My dad has the
same soft brown eyes
as my grandfather,
the same graying beard.

They built this house
together,
back in the '90s.

Well, they helped
build it with the
construction
company
they worked for.

But they don't
work there anymore.

Not for two years,
after Dad's boss
sent their team
a mass email:

I regret to inform you ...

After 20 years
on the job, my Dad
didn't get a raise or
paid vacation days.

He got a layoff letter.

He got overdue bills
and calls from
debt collectors.

He got problems
with the house that
we couldn't afford to fix.

He got into
even more fights
with my mom.

This time, about money:

> *We can't support
> our family on
> just my income,*
> Mom said.

> *What are we going
> to do, Dan?*

We still haven't
found an answer
to that question.

NOW SHOWING

But
once the light
from the TV screen

brightens
the dark basement,
it doesn't matter.

Not

my parents'
heavy silence,
then screaming.

Not

my dad's old boss
and my mom's
burning brisket.

Not

the missed calls
my sister never
answered.

> (The caller you
> are trying to reach
> is not available ...)

20

For now,

I am transported
onto another
planet.

  (A planet invaded
  by evil,
  which the

  hero will save
  in under
  90 minutes.)

INTERMISSION

Upstairs, I hear
the faint sound
of a car engine—

it rumbles and then
it's quiet.

The front door
swings open,

followed by a
chorus of voices:

Mom, Dad, and
Samantha.

Mom yells
from upstairs:

*ANNA, your
sister is here!*

I turn up the
the volume
on the remote

until their voices
sound more
like static.

SEEING SAMANTHA

Mom bangs on the door.

ANNA, NOW!
         Okay, Fine.

I walk up the stairs,
open the door,
and see her.

Samantha. My big sister.

Her hair is bleached
strawberry blond.

The curls we shared
have been straightened.

I touch my hair,
as if looking at hers
might make mine
disappear.

SURPRISE

But her hair isn't
the biggest shock.

I look down at
her belly

and

catch
my breath.

Like a
snag on
my sweater,
my words begin
to unravel.

You're pregnant?

LOOK

Why didn't
she call to tell me?

Did my parents
even know?

I look at Mom,
who's staring
down at her feet.

I look at Dad,
who rests a
gentle hand
on her shoulder.

I look back
at Samantha:
at her belly,
at her hair.

I turn around
and walk
downstairs.

DOWNPOUR

I can hear
the rain pouring
down in full force.

The basement feels
like the inside
of a freezer.

I press my ear to
the door and
hold my breath.

Samantha's voice
is soft, like a
librarian in a movie.

*Yeah, Mom, I packed
everything I need ...*

I imagine her
with glasses,
stacking books.

Little blue birds
fly around, like
in a Disney film.

*Anna doesn't seem
too happy to see me,*
she says.

When I hear my name,
the image disappears.

The birds fly away.
Suddenly, she's my
sister again.

For a moment,
the only sound
comes from the rain
hitting the roof.

Then, Mom's voice
cuts through, coarse
from a thousand
cigarettes.

She'll come around.

But she doesn't
sound convinced.

And neither
am I.

THEN ...

I hear footsteps.

I scramble
down the steps
right before
the door opens,

and I see
two pairs of feet:

Mom, followed
by Samantha.

INSPECTION

Samantha looks
wall to wall,

from the chipped
paint to the
faulty outlets.

Mom looks
up and down,

from the stained
carpet to the
popcorn ceiling.

I look between
the two of them,

who both can't
look at each other.

NEWS

I watch Samantha's eyes
scan the room.

Is she surprised to see
what's happened to
the house?

Mom clears
her throat, then says,

*Samantha will
be staying with you
in the basement
while we unpack
her old room.*

(*Our* old room
has been collecting
junk for three years.)

*You can sleep
on the couch for now,*
Mom says and
heads back upstairs.

APOLOGIES

Samantha gives me
a small smile.
An unspoken apology.

> Sorry you have to
> take the couch.

> Sorry there isn't
> a usable bedroom
> in this tiny house.

Maybe one day
she'll actually say,
I'm sorry.

> Sorry for leaving.
> Sorry for not calling.

> Sorry for forgetting
> about this family
> and starting a new one.

But for now,
she stays silent as
I grab my blanket.

RAGE

I pull the covers
over my head.
My breath is hot
beneath the blanket.

I try not to feel
the blanket
beneath my fists.

I try not to feel myself
twisting, twisting,
twisting the fabric.

I try not to notice
my hands shaking
from—what?

Shaking from
the cold

or

something
else?

WHEN I
WAKE UP

Samantha's blanket
is neatly folded
at the end of ~~my~~ her bed.

As if she never slept there.

THOUGHTS ON THE MORNING BUS RIDE

Coming-of-age films
show the shift
from youth to adulthood.

In most movies,
school is the center
of everything.

But let's be honest.

My high school isn't
any place you'd
choose to film.

My high school
has paint peeling off
the cinder blocks.

My high school
has overworked teachers,
ready to go on strike.

My high school
has kids who are seen
as problems, not prodigies.

My high school
is a place you'd rather
get in and get out.

MATH

I look up as
Aiden Wright
stumbles into
class, late
as usual.

Sorry,
he mutters
and slides onto
his chair.

Ms. Lopez
goes over the
math problems
on last night's
homework

while I review
a few problems
of my own:

Our family
-
Samantha
+
the pandemic
=
everything is
worse

36

COMPUTER LAB

While other kids
eat in the crowded
cafeteria,

I spend my
lunch hour alone,
watching YouTube.

Watching
video essays on
classic movies.

Watching
sneak peaks,
behind-the-scenes.

Watching
costume designers
explain their work.

Watching
anything to keep
from thinking about

Samantha.
Mom.
Dad.

IF I WORKED ON A MOVIE SET …

I'd want to be the DP:
the Director of
Photography.

Have you ever
watched a movie
and thought,

*How did they make
it look so good?*
Well, that's the DP.

The DP is the
secret weapon
in any great film.

The DP decides
what the cameras
should capture.

The DP knows
how to make a scene
worth watching.

The DP can make
any location
look beautiful.

IT TAKES A LOT TO MAKE A MOVIE

Sure, there are
the producers,
actors, and writers.

But then there
are the workers
below the line:

the DP, editors,
script supervisors,
and sound mixers.

(The names no one
bothers to read
once the credits roll.)

There are so many
jobs, so many
moving parts.

It's amazing that
most films don't
just fall apart.

FIVE SENSES

Dad drives me from
school to the video store.

What I see:
> The *check engine*
> light blinking.
> The gray sky.

What I smell:
> The pine
> air freshener,
> working overtime.

What I taste:
> Popcorn
> from lunch
> stuck in my teeth.

What I feel:
> My forehead
> pressed against
> the cool window.

What I hear:
> My dad's sigh.
> The tired engine.
> Nothing.

FAMILY HISTORY LESSON

Both my parents
grew up in families
that preferred silence.

They were never big
on birthdays,
holidays, or graduations.

They wouldn't offer a hug,
or say *I love you* much.

If Grandpa saw Mom
crying at his funeral, he
would have probably said,

> *Gee, Leah,*
> *don't get so emotional.*

My parents also
speak with as few
words as possible.

> *ANNA, are you home?*
> *ANNA, dinnertime!*
> *ANNA, do your homework.*

Unless they're fighting.
That's when they
won't hold back.

MEANING ...

We don't say *I love you*
at our house, either.

REWIND

Dad drops me off
in front of Rewind
and leaves without
saying goodbye.

Rewind is one of the
last video rental stores
in Pennsylvania.

Before Netflix and
Hulu, these stores
used to be
all over the place.

When I push open
the double doors,
I am transported
back 20 years.

The carpet is black
with neon spirals,
like it came out of
a '90s theater.

The walls are
covered with
posters of movies
hardly anyone
remembers.

I walk down the
rows of DVDs,
looking for
something new
to watch:

a great movie
tucked away in
a store that
feels like a
time capsule.

44

WHAT I KNOW ABOUT AIDEN WRIGHT

1.
He works the
cash register
at Rewind.

2.
We both played
soccer at the
rec center
in middle school.

3.
He sits behind me
in math class
(and spends most
of the time on
his phone).

4.
He never went to
any parties or football games,
even before the pandemic
had put things on pause.

5.
But if there
was a fight, you
know he'd be
there

with bruised fists
and blood
gushing out
his nose

and a smirk
on his face,
one that said:

Go ahead,
hit me again.

WHAT I KNOW ABOUT AIDEN WRIGHT, PT. 2

I know we've
never shared
more than a
couple of
sentences at the
cash register:

> *Would you like
> your receipt?*

> > *Yes, please.*

> *Have a nice
> evening.*

Or a few awkward moments
before the
bell rings in
math class:

> *You have
> an extra pencil?*

> > *Nah, sorry.*

> *No worries.*

47

So why are his
eyes burning
into my back?

CHECKOUT

That will be
two dollars and
twelve cents,
Aiden says.

I reach in
my pocket for
a couple
ragged bills.

When I look up,
he's staring down
at the register.

His curly bangs
block his eyes.

Now he can't
look at me
at all.

IN DEFENSE OF RENTING MOVIES

Yeah, I could
probably just pirate
the movie online.

Or stream it somewhere
for a few bucks.

But there's
something about
how the light
hits the disc.

How the DVD player
hisses and spits,

like it did
during family
movie nights
when I was little.

I hear the
familiar music
of Warner Brothers.

And everything
off-screen
falls silent.

RAIN

It's been storming
ever since
I got back home
from Rewind.

Mom used to
love the rain.
She said it was good
for her garden.

She would grow
her own carrots
to cut up and
serve with brisket.

Now
we only eat
brisket on
special occasions.

Now
she just buys
her carrots from
the supermarket.

I wonder,
if I closed my eyes,
could I taste
the difference?

ARGUMENTS

While I watch a movie,
a different scene
plays out upstairs.

My parents go
back and forth between
the same two fights.

Their words sound rehearsed,
like they've come from
a well-worn script.

They know their lines.
They've been off-book
for years.

FIRST FIGHT:

What's going on with Anna?

Dad's answer:

*She's just being a teenager—
too cool for her parents.*

Mom's answer:

*She's depressed. Maybe she
should talk to someone.*

Dad:

We can't afford it.

Mom:

Silence.

TALK TO SOMEONE?

*Maybe she should
talk to someone,*
Mom had said.

Right. *I* should
talk to someone,
but who talks to me?

Not Mom. Not Dad.
Not Samantha.

> Yeah, yeah.
> I get it.

I know what she
really means:

That I should see
a therapist
or take medication
with a bunch of
side effects.

But no therapist
could change
this place.

Maybe it's my
family that needs help.

Maybe it's the
world around me—

not just me.

SECOND FIGHT

Like always, their fight
becomes about the house.

*What do we do about
the house falling apart?*

> Mom's answer:

> *We need to stop
> spending all our money
> trying to save
> this house.*

> Dad's answer:

> *A few cracks in the walls
> never hurt anyone.*

> Mom:

> *This house is a
> sinking ship and
> we're drowning with it.*

> Dad:

> Silence.

BAD MOVIE

Hearing my
parents argue
is like watching
a bad movie
again and again.

You know
how it's going
to end.

But every time
you watch,
you feel
disappointed.

SAMANTHA SPEAKS

That's something
I didn't miss.

I pause the TV
and turn around
to see Samantha
standing behind
the couch.

She's holding
two shopping bags.
I see baby clothes and
diapers peeking out
from the plastic.

She lowers her eyes.
I had hoped they'd
stop fighting.
I couldn't stand it
when I was sixteen.

Now I'm the one
who's sixteen and
can't wait to leave.

I SPEAK

It's only
gotten worse
since the pandemic.

Dad lost his job,
you know.

Samantha sighs,
eyes glued to
the ground.

Yeah, I know.
Mom told me
when I got here.

I turn around
and stare into
the screen.

Out of the corner
of my eye,
I see her

tiptoe around
the couch,
like one wrong step

will send her
crashing through
the floor.

She takes a seat.
So what are
you watching?

OKAY

We don't talk.
We just watch.

And I feel

kind of,
sort of,
maybe

okay with it.

BACK AT REWIND

Between racks of
dusty DVDs,
I find a couple
romantic comedies
I haven't seen.

Aiden stares
as I walk toward
the register.

What's your problem?
I think, and—wow,
did I say that out loud?

Aiden's eyes widen.
He tries to speak.
You're just, you know ...

I raise my eyebrows.
I'm what, exactly?

Nothing, nothing,
he says, looking down
at the plastic cases.
So, uh, is this one good?
I don't watch a lot
of romance.

I cross my arms.
What do you watch then?

His eyes light up.
Horror. Have you
seen Footprints in
the Garden?

No. I don't do gore.

He pauses.
Fair enough.
But you should
give it a chance.

He pulls a DVD
from under the counter.
On the house.

I look around,
waiting for the owner
to pop out of thin air
and bust us.

Can you do that?

He shrugs and
scribbles his
number on a
scrap of receipt paper.

*Text me when
you're finished.*

Our fingers brush
just for a second
as I take the paper
from him.

*Okay. I'll tell you
how much
I hated it,* I say.

64

TOGETHER

Samantha sits,
legs crossed,
on the carpet.

I see her stuff
spread out
all around
the basement.

We're sharing
a room again,

but this time
she feels more
like stranger
and less like
my sister.

On TV,
a woman with
perfect teeth
talks about the
best stretches
to do in your
second trimester.

Samantha smiles
when she
sees me
hanging out

on the steps,
halfway in
and halfway out
of the basement.

Wanna join?
she asks.
It's kinda fun.

You've got to
be kidding me.
This is
my basement,
my TV.

My place away
from everyone,
everything.

My muscles
tense.

I feel like
a wind-up toy
with my gears
being
tightened.

But for some
reason, I still
go sit
next to her.

JUST BREATHE?

The woman
on the screen
says to take
a deep breath.

Count to four,
now do it
again!

How can I
breathe in
and out

when my
breath is
always shallow,

scared to take in
too much
oxygen?

Scared that
if I finally
let myself
huff and puff,

I'll blow this
whole house
down.

INT. LIVING ROOM – DAY

The door to the basement SLAMS open.

ANNA runs through the living room

... and pulls the curtains down.

SMASH! She throws a rock at the window

... and glass shatters everywhere.

ANNA KICKS the four walls again and
again

... until they CRACK and fall over.

THUD. The house has split open.

ACT TWO

HORROR MOVIE

When Samantha
heads upstairs,
I watch the movie
Aiden lent me.

Footprints in the Garden
sounds more like
a fairy tale, less
like horror.

(Until you realize
the footprints are
from a monster
that murdered the
gardener.)

I have to admit:
the camera work is
brilliant.

When the credits roll,
I'm sad that
it's over.

I TEXT AIDEN

I watched
your movie.
It was better
than I expected.

Seconds later,
my phone rings
with a response.

See! You had to
give it a chance.

And then,
another text:
one that makes
my heart flutter
in fear, or maybe
excitement.

You should join
my film club.

We meet
every Sunday
on Zoom.
Ya know,
if you want to.

I text back:

Yeah ok.
Send me the link.

I pause,
and then I
type out,

Thanks.

PROBLEM CHILD

The fights begin
again: reruns of
the same program.

Anna. Anna. Anna.
The house. The house.
The house. The house.

Between the two of us,
there's no competition.

The house is the
true problem child.

More of a nuisance
than Samantha or I
could ever be.

Trust me—
if these walls
could talk, they'd
be screaming.

LET GO

My family
used to watch
movies together.

One night,
when I was still
in middle school,
we watched *Titanic.*

(Mom whispered
Oh my and covered
my eyes during
the sex scene.)

Dad couldn't
believe that Rose
threw her jeweled
necklace back
into the ocean.

That makes no sense.
Why would she
get rid of it?

He couldn't see
that sometimes
the best thing to do
is let something go.

FILM CLUB

My heart pounds
as I stare at my
dad's computer screen.

I've been sitting in
the Zoom waiting room,
waiting and waiting.

For what? To meet
a bunch of Aiden's
weird friends?

Guys who love *Fight Club*
and can only speak
with their fists?

This was a mistake.
I should sign off.
Leave.

But before I can hit
the X in the corner
of the screen,

the Zoom host
lets me into
Aiden's world.

There are only four
people in film club,
four squares on my screen.

And none of them
are who I assumed
they would be.

> There's Riley,
> with pink hair and
> cat-eye glasses.

> They want to be
> a Prop Master
> for television

> and know how
> to make a
> fake cigarette
> out of paper and
> dried parsley.

> *It's really easy!*
> *I could show you*
> *sometime.*

There's Justin,
who has a
Lord of the Rings
poster on his door.

He tells me
about fantasy lore

and says I
should check out
the graphics

on his favorite
video game,
Bloodborne.

*The visual storytelling
is amazing!*

There's Rosa,
with a smile
that brightens
my screen
by 100 watts.

She believes
that Romance
should be taken
just as seriously
as any genre

and has very strong
opinions about
The Notebook.

*It's not even close
to Ryan Gosling's
best work.*

Then of course,
there's Aiden, who
loves horror.

If you liked
Footprints,
you should
check out the sequel ...

Aiden, who I
can't believe
is making me
appreciate movies
with blood and guts.

Aiden, who
looks kind of cute
when he talks.

SPECIAL, PT. 1

There must be
something special
about the people here.

Or maybe there's
something special
about this space.

I start to say
things I would never
mention in front
of my family,

    like

    I love the sound
    of a disc when it
    pops out of the case

    and

    When a good movie
    ends, I feel sad, like
    I've lost something.

I raise my hand to
my lips, scared
I said too much.

But they smile
and ask questions.

They talk and then
they listen.

SPECIAL, PT. 2

Maybe a space like that
shouldn't be so special.

Special, as in, rare.

STRESS

Our water pipes
aren't working (again).

Dad drives us to
the grocery store

to brush our teeth
in their bathroom.

Mom stares at
Samantha's belly

as she spits
into the sink.

The woman from the
exercise video

said stress is bad
during pregnancy.

I wonder if we are
thinking the same thing.

SMOKE

I follow Mom
out of the bathroom,
to the front of
the store.

I watch as she
leans against the wall
and lights a
cigarette.

Can you experience
secondhand stress?

It feels like I'm
choking on it.

I ASK DAD TO DRIVE ME TO REWIND

Because
I need to return
Footprints before
the owner realizes it's gone.

Because
there's nothing to do
if I can't find anything
worth watching in my room.

Because
I love my basement, but
I'm getting a little tired
of squashing spiders.

Because
I want to get to know
the guy who made me feel
something like hope.

AT REWIND

I slide the disc
across the counter.
*I'm here to return
stolen merchandise.*

He brushes his bangs
from his eyes.
I see his knuckles—
all red and swollen.

I'm about to clock out,
he says. *Do you
want to take a walk
around town?*

WE WALK DOWN MAIN STREET

Past the brick buildings
with historic plaques.

Around the antique stores
and diner (open 24 hours).

We stroll through the park,
crowded with oak trees.

The fallen leaves crunch
under our sneakers

as we wander toward
nothing in particular.

WHAT I LEARN ABOUT AIDEN WRIGHT

1.
He lives
around the corner
from our school.

2.
His mom wants him
to go to college, since
she never did.

3.
He posts movie reviews
on TikTok, but is too
embarrassed to show me.

4.
He hates the
greasy taste of popcorn,
but has a sweet tooth.

5.
He isn't dating anyone
and wonders
why I ask.

I HAVE ANOTHER QUESTION

How do you ask
about bruised knuckles?

Do you try to be
as polite as possible?

*(Parden me, but I noticed
your fists are red and purple.)*

Instead, I go with a joke:

*So what, are you, like, a
bad boy in a teen movie?*

ANSWER

For a moment
I think he's offended.

But then he laughs
like a lion's roar:
unafraid to be heard.

Nah, I'm not
the main character
in some
coming-of-age film.

I smile.
Oh really?
No dark backstory?
No broken home life?

He shrugs and says,
Not any more
dark or broken
than anyone else's.

I live with my mom.
She's great.
My dad left a
long time ago.

He pauses and
his smile fades.

My mom's sick.
The pandemic
was really hard.

I couldn't stand
feeling so angry,
so scared for her.

He looks down at
his knuckles.

And as you've
probably heard,
I've never been
good with anger.

BACKSTORY

We sit among
the dead leaves
as Aiden tells me
his backstory.

He says he started
fighting when
he was a kid,
after his dad left.

A shove
on the playground
turned into
something more.

He said
one time:

He broke another
kid's nose.
He gave another guy
a black eye.

He's not proud
of his fights, like
some other guys.

(The ones that brag
about how much
weight they can lift
in gym class.)

He knows that
he shouldn't
be picking fights.

So he's trying to
*get better at
controlling his anger ...*

(At least that's
what he tells all
the social workers
and counselors.)

But how can
you control a rage
that feels so
justified?

How can you
stop and breathe
when you feel like
once you open
your mouth,
you'll scream?

WEIGHT

My fingers trace
through the
grass

as Aiden explains
why he started
film club:

It's a new type
of escape.

It's a way to
meet people who
also need a break.

*I still care about
the hard stuff: the
money, my mom,*

*but I need to find
a better way
to deal.*

I pick up a rock
caked with dirt,
heavy in my palm.

I guess anger
is a little like
cradling

a million
of these rocks
in your arms.

Not knowing
where to put
them down.

Not knowing
if you can

carry the weight

or if the stones
will fall out of
your grip.

One by
one by
one.

AM I ANGRY?

I throw the rock
and watch
as it disappears
into a pile
of leaves.

His words hit
something deep
in my chest.

My own feeling
I'd rather ignore
and forget.

       Am I angry?
       I'm afraid to be.

But maybe
I am already.

A LIST OF EVERYTHING I MIGHT BE ANGRY AT

- The house
- My dad for keeping the house
- My mom for ignoring me
- Samantha for disappearing
- This town for making everything gray
- The world for not being just a bit fair

LITTLE FIRE

Back home,
I find Samantha
sitting in the
living room.

Her red sweater
is stretched tight
around her belly.

She flips through
a paperback.

What's that?
I ask.

She looks up.
*It's some old
baby name book
Mom gave me.*

I sit down
next to her
on the couch.

*What does the name
Samantha mean?*
I ask.

She checks
the table of contents
to find the *S* section.

Samantha
comes from the
Hebrew word
for Listener
of God.

I remember her
as a preteen,
rolling her eyes

the few times
Mom made us
go to synagogue.

(The closest one
is an hour away.
Practicing religion
was only for
special occasions.)

I don't think
that suits you, I say.

Samantha shrugs.
Sometimes a name
is just a name.

What about
the name Aiden?
I ask.

She flips back
to the first few
pages and
squints down.

*Aiden means
Little Fire.*

Yeah, sounds
about right.

SAMANTHA
BEGINS TO CRY

It starts softly,
a whimper.
So quiet I can
barely hear it.

Then, it pours,
louder than
the rain hitting
the roof.

I can't do this.
I can't be
a good mom.

I can't even
be a good
older sister.

I can't even
be a good
adult.

I can't—I can't—

Before I realize
what I'm
doing,

I wrap my arms
around her
shoulders.

Her blond hair
falls against
my chest

as she cries
into the sleeve of
my T-shirt.

All I can think
to say is,

*You don't have
to be anything
right now, okay?*

UNDERSTAND

I hate that
Samantha left,
but I understand.

I understand
what it's like
to want
to drive off
into the sunset.

To let go of all
the bad feelings
and pretend

that the good
ones never
have to end.

UGLY TRUTH

You remember Trey?
she asks.
How could I forget?

Trey: her boyfriend
from high school
who she drove off with.

She wipes her eyes
on her sweater sleeve.
Well, he left me.

Oh.
Scratch that.
Her ex-boyfriend.

He proposed after
we found out
I was pregnant.

But last month,
he changed his mind,
said he didn't want kids.

That's why I came
back here.
I just needed—

SUPPORT

She stops,
looks down at
the baby book.

She doesn't
need to say
another word.

I know what
she means.

TREY BANKS:

Her boyfriend
turned fiancé.
Turned ex-fiancé.

Who turned out
to be the devil.

I shake my head.
That's messed up.

She sighs and rests
her head on my
shoulder.

Yeah, it is, she says.
*Thanks for being
the first person
to say that.*

YOU CAN QUOTE ME

*A lot of stuff
is pretty messed up.*

- Anna, the philosopher

NIGHTTIME

I'm lying on the
couch, staring at the
popcorn ceiling.

What I've learned
from HGTV home
makeover shows:

A popcorn ceiling
is a ceiling with
a type of spray

that creates a rough,
bumpy texture
(like popcorn).

It's used as a cheap
way to cover up
imperfections.

If you chipped away
the paint, what flaws
would you find?

2 A.M. THOUGHTS:

1.
I don't trust
the support beams
holding up this house.

2.
I don't think
my parents know
how to support us.

3.
Honestly,
popcorn ceilings
are really ugly.

4.
I need to focus on
something other than
what's breaking.

5.
What should I talk
about at film club
on Sunday?

SUNDAY

Riley, Justin,
Rosa, Aiden, and I

talk about
the movies we
watched over the
weekend:

> *Have you all*
> *seen* Parasite?
> *It blew my mind,*
> Aiden says.

We talk about
film styles
and Oscar
nominations.

But we also
just chat:

About music.
About politics.
About our
family and friends.

> *I started taking*
> *dance lessons*
> *at the rec center,*
> Riley shares.

And honestly,
It's nice to have
people to talk to,

even if I don't
share much about
my own family
and (lack of) friends.

I learn that
Justin has an
action figure
collection.

> *Super nerdy,*
> *I know,* he says.
> But I think it
> sounds cool.

I learn that
Riley and Rosa
are both
homeschooled.

That's why I haven't
seen them around.

And I thought
I had already
seen everything
in this town.

FILM PROJECT

Riley has been
filming around town,
capturing
the spirit of Garey,
as they put it.

How will you find
anything to film?
It's kind of
drab here, I say.

Riley shrugs.
Yeah, it can be.

But I like the horses
and antique stores,
the rolling hills
and farmers markets.

Plus, there are
some pretty cool
people here,
if you look for them.

LOCATION

Aiden asks,
Have you seen
The Sixth Sense?

I nod. Who hasn't?
That was one
of the few thrillers
I had already seen
before Aiden
introduced me
to scary movies.

Well, that was shot
in Philly—a couple
hours from here.

Rosa chimes in:
So was Silver Linings
Playbook!

Plus, there are
enough films shot
in places like
New York City and
Hollywood,
adds Justin.

Maybe there's
something here
we can show them.

MEMORY

I remember when
Mom and Dad
took Samantha
and me on a trip
to Pittsburgh.

I was 10 and
Samantha was
15—
right before we
stopped being close.

Neither of us
was planning on
leaving town
(not just yet).

That was only
six years ago,
but six years
feel like forever.

Mom paid
five bucks for
each of us
to ride up the
Duquesne Incline.

At first, I was
disappointed
when I learned

that we'd be
slowly rising
up the track
instead of
flying fast, like a
roller coaster.

But then,
we boarded the
cable car. We were
slowly lifted
up the mountain,
into the sky.

And I saw
the beautiful
city skyline
mixed with
rolling hills.

It was something
out of a DP's
dream.

So okay, fine.
There are views
I remember
worth capturing
on camera.

Maybe even
a few here,
in Garey,
Pennsylvania.

CROSS-FADE

Aiden ends the
Zoom meeting,
and just like that,

one scene
fades out and
another fades in:

A scene
I'd rather not
witness.

ACTION!

If my life was a movie,
and I was the DP,

This is how I would
shoot the scene ...

> INTO FRAME
> Samantha,
>
> who runs down
> the basement stairs,
> screaming:
>
> *Stop trying to*
> *change my mind.*
> *I can't do this alone!*
>
> She yanks open
> the dresser drawer
>
> and starts throwing
> her clothes into
> an empty suitcase.

PAN TO
Mom,

rushing
right behind her,

stairs creaking
beneath her feet.

I'm not letting
you move back
with him.
Not after what
you've told me,
she says,
catching her breath.

You're not alone.
We're here to—

      PULL FOCUS
      to Samantha,

      who cuts Mom off
      before she can finish.

      Her words sound
      as sharp as
      a steak knife:

      Support me?
      You and Dad are
      the reason I left
      in the first place.

      All you care
      about is fighting.

CLOSE ON
Mom.

I can't tell
what she's feeling
from her face.

She stands there,
stone cold.
Not moving.
Barely blinking.

>PULL BACK
>to see me,
>
>with my laptop
>half-closed
>and my mouth
>wide open.
>
>I'm stuck between
>being part of
>the scene
>and part of
>the audience.

THE TRUTH IS

My head is not
a camera.

My eyes are not
lenses.

My mouth is not
a microphone.

My mom and
sister are not actors.

I am not the
director, in control.

Not even close.

FREEZE FRAME

When Samantha's
words drop, Mom
stops in her tracks.

For a moment,
everything
is put on pause
and the world
becomes still,
like a photograph.

Samantha holds
a fist full of clothes
like a weapon.

I sit still
behind my desk,
holding my breath.

Mom breaks
the silence:

*Can you wait
until tomorrow?*

*Then you can
go back to him.
You can leave.*

I watch
Samantha's fingers

twist the fabric
in her hands—

the same thing
I do when I try
to calm down.

Then, she
releases the shirts,
lets them fall to
the floor.

*Okay. I'll stay
the night.*

Her voice is
calm again.
But she doesn't
put her clothes
back in the dresser.

She leaves her
suitcase hanging
wide open,
like a threat.

A reminder
that she could
leave again
at any moment.

When Mom leaves,
Samantha looks at me.

Clenched jaw.
Flushed red.

Don't say anything, Anna.
I can't deal with it right now.

I close Dad's laptop
and stand up.

Legs shaking.
Mouth dry.

I don't have anything
to tell you, anyway,
I say.

WHAT I KNOW ABOUT TREY BANKS:

1.
He grew up
in one of the biggest
houses in town.

2.
He probably never
had to worry about
credit card bills.

3.
He once spit
my Mom's brisket
into a napkin.

4.
He once said
I was *not as pretty
as Samantha.*

5.
He left his
pregnant fiancée
(AKA, my sister).

6.
He's a jerk
who doesn't deserve
a redemption arc.

OUTSIDE

The cold air
hits my skin
as I look up at
the gray sky.

The brown grass
is like sandpaper
under the soles
of my feet.

I wish our grass
was bright green,
like summertime
in California.

I wish I never
had to walk
back inside
this broken house.

I wish I didn't
have to sleep
next to the spiders,
near my sister.

Maybe it would
have been better
if she never
came back.

I don't think
we can deal
with any more
damage.

I SEE MOM OUTSIDE (FROM THREE CAMERA ANGLES)

Long shot:

> From a distance,
> she only looks like
> the shape of a person.
>
> Hunched over, head
> in her hands.
> Her hair (curly, like mine)
> is pushed to the side.

Medium shot:

> When the camera
> cuts closer, you can
> see her cigarette.
>
> She doesn't bring it
> to her lips.
> The ash falls as
> her frown lines deepen.

Close-up shot:

 The camera closes in
 on her tired eyes
 as she does something
 my mom rarely does:

 Cry.

CRY

I've only seen Mom cry
a handful of times:

> When my
> grandpa died.

> When she broke
> her wrist.

> When
> Samantha left.

But tonight, she
sits on the grass
and sobs.

It's the most
powerful sound
I've ever heard.

I can't believe it,
but I'd rather hear
her fight with dad.

I'd rather hear
anything else.

TEXTS TO AIDEN, LEFT ON READ

Hey.

You there?

*Everything is
falling apart.*

My sister is leaving.

*My parents
can't handle it.*

*I don't think I
can handle it.*

Can we talk?

Hello?

*Fine, whatever.
Don't respond.*

EXT. HOUSE – DAY

Anna stands in the middle of a destroyed house. She is alone. She looks around, confused. Where has everyone gone?

                    ANNA

          Hello? Is anyone here?

Anna looks up at us.

                    ANNA (CONT'D)
                    (to the camera)

          I don't want to film this
              scene by myself.

Anna looks around the rubble.

                    ANNA (CONT'D)

          What if everything is broken
                beyond repair?

Anna screams, but nobody hears.

ACT THREE

THE NEXT DAY

It's weird to go
to school when the
world feels like
it's crumbling
around you.

I sit at my desk.
I don't raise
my hand.
I don't answer
questions.

Until ...

some girl in
English class
won't stop playing
videos on her phone
without earbuds.

And some guy
keeps leering at
my chest and
joking around with
his friends.

And I can't
focus on the
teacher, or my
textbook, or my
own thoughts.

And finally,
I yell,

*WILL YOU
ALL JUST
SHUT UP?*

EXHAUSTED

I get sent to
the school counselor.

She asks all the
right questions.

*What's going on
with you, Anna?*

She tilts her head
and pretends to
look concerned.

She says again
and again
that she
*really wants to
help me.*

I'm too tired
to play along,
to answer her
questions.

I'm too tired
for any of this.

But then, I feel
my stomach churn
with anger.

And I borrow
a bit of
Aiden's fire.

I stare her
in the eyes
and say:

*What I need
is more money
for my parents
to fix our house
and get out
of debt.*

*What I need
is support
for my pregnant
sister, whose
boyfriend is
the worst.*

*What I need
is to stop
feeling so
depressed,
so hopeless.*

*Can you help me
with that?*

I hardly
recognize
my own voice.

It sounds as
razor-sharp
as Samantha's
was last night.

The counselor
presses her
lips together.

Silence.

DETENTION

My so-called
snide remarks
land me in detention.

Funny, because
I thought I was finally
speaking the truth.

But I guess
I didn't tell her what
she wanted to hear.

(Easy answers, like,
I'm fine! Just stressed
about homework.
That's all!)

After seventh period,
I head to the
auditorium

to sit with the
bad kids—the kids
who can't sit down
and shut up.

The kids who
have a little fire
in them.

... and guess who I see?

AIDEN

Aiden lies across the
bleachers, looking
at his phone.

Nothing seems to
distract him from
the screen—

Not the sound of
the stressed-out teacher
on detention duty,

arguing with one of
the kids from my
English class.

Or the girl behind him
who won't stop
giggling on the phone.

(Yeah, yeah—
HAHAHA!
Oh my gosh—I know!)

But once he sees
me, he sits up.
He slides his phone
in his pocket.

He looks at me
the way he did
back when we first
started talking
at Rewind.

Back then, I thought
he was glaring,
but now I see

he looks like
he actually wants
to talk with me.

RUDE

What are you
doing here?
he asks.

I'm not in the
mood to explain.
So I ask my
own question:

Why didn't you text
me back last night?
I cross my arms.
It was pretty rude.

Aiden sighs and
runs his fingers
through his hair.

I don't know.
I'm sorry.
I just—I have a lot
to deal with, too.

Now *I* feel
like the one who
was being rude.

HELP

You know how
people say:

*You have to
help yourself
before you can
help others.*

That can be
good advice
sometimes,
but maybe
it's not always
true.

Maybe we
don't have to
to have it
all together
to support
one another.

(I mean,
isn't that
asking a lot?)

I sit beside Aiden.

142

This time
I only ask
one question:

What can I do?

AIDEN'S ANSWER:

Just getting it
is enough.
Thanks, Anna.

There's no
touching allowed
in detention.

That would feel
more like comfort,
less like
punishment.

But Aiden
holds my hand
under the
bleacher seats.

I feel his knuckles
rest under my
fingertips.

His wounds
have started
to smooth over.

Meanwhile,
mine feel like
they've started
to split open.

THEN HE SAYS:

*What can I do
to help you?*

My answer:

*Just don't stop
holding my hand.*

And for the rest
of the afternoon,
he doesn't.

A LIST OF EVERYTHING I MIGHT BE ANGRY AT (UPDATED)

- The house

(Or maybe I'm angry
that the house is
something we have
to worry about
in the first place.)

- My dad

(Or maybe I'm angry
at my dad's boss
for firing him.
For making things
so unfair.)

- My mom

(Or maybe I'm angry
that my mom tries
her best, but doesn't
know how to say
I love you back.)

146

- Samantha

(Or maybe I'm angry
that she left. That she
wasn't there for me
while everything
was falling apart.)

- This town

(Or maybe I'm angry
that no one taught me
how to find
beauty in a place
that isn't perfect.)

HEIRLOOM

I think this anger
is something
my family shares:

something we
don't talk about,
but we feel,
thick in the air.

Maybe that's
why it's easier
to be mad
than to say:

I love you.
I understand.
I'm sorry.

PARKING LOT

Aiden and I
walk out of
detention together,
holding hands.

Outside, I see
Dad's beat-up car
sitting in the
parking lot.

Aiden rides off
on his bike as I
slide into the
passenger's seat.

*How long have you
been waiting here?*
I ask Dad.

He rubs his beard
and looks down at
his watch.

*Oh, um.
I'm not sure.
Maybe an hour.*

*Your mom and I
saw that you didn't
come home on
the bus.*

*I wanted to
make sure you had
someone here to
pick you up.*

LOVE

Dad's car engine
wheezes as we
drive down the road.

We sit in silence,
until I tell Dad why
I didn't come home.

I got detention.
I'm sorry.
Am I in trouble?

When we stop
at the red light,
Dad turns his head.

He gives me
a small smile,
the kind that says:

> There's enough
> to worry about
> already, isn't there?

I guess that's one way
to say *I love you*
without saying it.

FOCUS

When I get home,
Samantha and Mom
are sitting in the
living room.

I go downstairs
and switch on the TV.

As far as I turn up
the volume, I can't
focus on the screen.

The characters' mouths
move, but I don't
hear anything.

> Is Samantha going
> to disappear again?

Last night, I wished
she never came back.

But now, the thought of
losing her again

scares me more
than any movie
Aiden could lend me.

HOLDING
MY BREATH

For too long,
I've been holding
my breath.
I've been holding
my anger in.

I've been keeping
my feelings
locked up, like
caged animals.

Scared to release
them into the wild.
Worried they might
break what is
so fragile.

That being said ...

there are perks
to knowing how
to hold your breath
and listen.

I hold my ear
against the basement
door, trying to hear
what Samantha is
saying to Mom.

But their voices
are too quiet.
Everything
sounds muffled.

I can only pick up
bits and pieces:

... yeah, I know ...

... I just ... okay ...

... do you even ...

And I'm left with
more questions
than answers.

TALK

After an eternity,
Samantha comes
downstairs and
sits next to me.

I can see the roots
of her hair
creeping out from
under the dye:

the hair that used
to look so much
like mine.

Will she ever let
it grow back again?

Or will she leave
it blonde forever?

I'm sorry, she says.
*I'm sorry I left
and didn't call.*

*I'm sorry I was
about to do it
all over again.*

She shakes her head—
At me? Or maybe
at herself.

*I'm sorry you
had to see me
snap at Mom.
It was my fault.*

*We got into a fight
about Trey—*

She pauses,
then says,

*All this stuff can
get overwhelming
sometimes.*

*I don't always have
the right answer.
But I'm trying.*

SORRY

When I
finally hear
Samantha say it,

I feel my body
relax, like I had
been holding

stress in my
shoulders without
realizing it.

It's amazing how
just a couple
small words

can feel so
important.

ME TOO

I'm sorry, too,
is all I say.

But there's
so much more
I could mention.

There are so many
missed moments
from the last
three years:

times we could
have both told
each other
how we felt,
but didn't.

A whole perfect script.

Maybe one day
it will be easier
to talk things
through.

But for now,
I'm sorry
is enough.

PLOT HOLE

You know what's funny?
she says all of a sudden.

Last night, I was so mad.
I just wanted to drive off.

But then I remembered
this morning that

Dad drove me here.
I don't have a car anymore.

Samantha throws her
head back and laughs.

I mean—she continues,
catching her breath.

That kind of puts a damper
on my dramatic exit.

And I start laughing, too.

Because life's not like
the movies.

Sometimes, it's funnier.

I WANT TO ASK...

Why was Mom
so angry about Trey?

Does she know
something I don't?

But I figure that's
not for me to know.
Not just yet.

Not until Samantha
is ready to share.

So instead, I ask,
*Do you want to
watch a movie?*

Samantha smiles.
How about a musical?
Those are my favorite.

DECEMBER

Today is the first
day of December.

Around town,
people have
pulled out their
dusty boxes
marked *CHRISTMAS*.

Their houses are
decorated with
bright lights
and blow-up
snowmen.

It's nice out there,
Samantha says,
peering out
the window.

Our front yard
is covered in
a thin sheet of white.

Remember when
we used to surprise
each other with
snowball fights?
she asks.

I laugh.

Yeah. We'd even
throw them
in the house.

(Dad wasn't
too happy about that.)

I check the clock.

It's about time to
start my long walk
to the bus stop.

I grab my backpack
and head outside.

And then ...

I feel something
thud against
my puffy coat.
A snowball.

I turn around.
Samantha waves
from the porch
with ice on
her fingers.

LITTLE TALKS

I meet Aiden
outside of Rewind.

We walk along
the sidewalk,
helping each other
hop over
the icy parts.

We talk about
his mom and
my mom,
his dad and
my dad.

We talk about
Samantha
and her baby
on the way.

We talk about
movies and
film club and
winter break.

We talk about
math class and
TikTok and
getting detention.

And in these
little talks,
everything feels
easy.

COLD

We stop to rest
at the park.

A month ago
we sat here
and had our first
real talk.

The days are
starting to get
shorter and
shorter.

It's only
4:45 p.m. and
the sun is about
to set.

But I don't want
this day to end,
not yet.

Aiden's cheeks
and nose are
flushed red
from the cold.

But he smiles
and says,
I love winter.

My curls stick
to the side of
my face,
damp from the
falling snowflakes.

Aiden reaches
for my hand.

His fingers feel
like little icicles
(mine do too, I bet).

But I don't mind
the cold.

I don't mind
it at all.

MAGIC HOUR

It's magic hour,
Aiden says.

In filmmaking,
magic hour
is that perfect
moment

right when
the sun rises
or right when
the sun sets.

When it's not
too dark, not
too bright.

It's the
best time
to film.

And maybe
the best time
to take a risk.

I lean forward.
He leans forward.

Finally,
we kiss.

RETAKE

I look at him.

At the snowflakes
in his eyelashes.

At the corners of
his lips, curving up.

There's no need
for a redo.

That first take
was perfect.

But I want to capture
this feeling

as often as I can
with Aiden.

*Can we do that
again?* I ask.

And we do.
Again and
again.

ANGER

In film club,
we talk about
our favorite
action scenes.

In Hollywood,
sometimes actors
will do push-ups
to get their
blood boiling
before a big
blowout.

But everyone
probably
has something
that burns from
their core—

something
they're already
angry about.

If you were
acting out a
fight scene, what
would you use
to get angry?
I ask.

At first, all I hear
is the faint hiss
of my laptop fan.

Surprisingly, Rosa
is the first
to speak up.

*Ooh, I'd probably
think about my
Mom's job.*

*She has to
work through
chronic pain
because her job
won't allow her
more sick days.*

Justin says,

*I'd remember
the things
people said
about me back in
middle school.*

Riley goes next:

*I'd think about
injustice.*

How there are
people out there
who wish
people like me
didn't exist.

But if I didn't
want to get
too angry, I'd
just do
the push-ups.

ROCKS

Before I know it,
I start to speak.

*Sometimes I feel
like I'm carrying
all these heavy
rocks in my hands.*

(My sister.
My parents.
Our house.)

*And I don't know
how to keep them
from weighing
me down.*

Four faces
look back at me.
Four people who
know exactly
what I mean.

Well, Rosa says,
*Now you have
other people to
help carry it
with you.*

I see myself
in the corner
of the screen,
tears running
down my cheeks.

I wipe my eyes.
This is the first
time I've cried
in a while.

But they're
not sad tears.

I feel lighter,
relieved.

Like I really was
carrying rocks
and someone
just took a few
of them from me.

I finally let out
the longest,
deepest
breath.

LAUGHTER

We stay silent
for a moment,
soaking in everything
just spoken.

Hey, Aiden,
you didn't share,
Justin points out.

Aiden sighs, and
looks down at
his keyboard.

I guess I'm angry
that I don't know
what to do with all
this anger.

I let out another
deep breath.
That one
hit me hard.

Isn't it obvious
what you should do?
Riley says.

Aiden looks up.
No. What?

Fight,
they answer.

You know
I'm trying not
to do that anymore,
he says.
His voice wavers,
like a shaky cam.

Riley shakes
their head.
No, not like that.

I mean, use your
anger to fight
for things to
get better.

The corners of
his lips curve up
from a frown
to a grin.

He slaps his
hand on his head.
Oh yeah, of course.

He starts to laugh
and then we
all join in.

After all the anger,
laughter feels
really good
right now.

A LIST OF EVERYONE I THINK I LOVE

- Mom
- Dad
- Samantha
- Her baby (once she comes)
- My new friends
- Aiden

EMBRACE

I walk upstairs
and see Mom
sitting on the couch.

I wrap my arms
around her
shoulders.

I feel her body
twitch beneath
my touch.

I love you, Mom.

She squeezes
my arms,
like a half-hug.

This is the way
my mom says
I love you, too.

DECISIONS

Samantha decides
to stay for
a few months
after the baby comes.

Trey hasn't called
and she doesn't
plan on reaching out,
at least for now.

She has other people
she can lean on.

TONIGHT

My parents fight.

Okay, I guess
everything can't
change within
just a few days.

In a movie it
would, but not
in the real world.

They argue about:

*The house. The house.
The house. The house.*

But this time, the
script flips.

Mom stops yelling
for a second.

She takes a deep
breath and
finally says,

*I understand this
is hard for you, Dan.
I'm sorry.*

I'm only trying to

think of what's best
for our family.

I know you're
trying to do the same.

With those
little words,

my mom must have
broken something—

broken,
in a good way.

She shattered an
invisible wall
Dad had been
holding up.

(A wall
that was stronger
than the real walls
in this house.)

He cries and says,

I know, Leah,
I know.

At least for tonight,
the fighting
is finally over.

GROW

I hate hearing
my dad cry.

I wish things
could have been
different.

I wish we could
crawl into a
movie scene

and not
have to face
this reality.

But maybe this
is the type
of pain

that good things
can grow from.

FRIEND

I ask Mom if
I can invite a friend
over to the house.

Her eyebrows rise
as she opens and
closes her mouth.

Oh, really? she says,
surprised but not
upset. *Who is it?*

I bite my lip.
Uh, Aiden Wright.

Everyone
around town
has heard about
Aiden's fights.

Oh, she says.
*I know his mom.
Nice woman.
I should call her.*

That's the thing
about living in
a small town.

My mom knows
everyone's mom.

But for the
first time since
starting middle school,
this doesn't make
me cringe.

In fact, I think
it's kind of cool
to feel so ...
connected.

*Would you like me
to make a brisket?*
Mom asks.

I bite my lip.
Can we afford it?

Mom is quiet
for a moment.
Then she says,

*I'm not going
to lie to you, Anna.
We'll be facing
a lot of tough
challenges.*

*But for tonight,
I don't want you
to worry about
the finances.*

Let your dad
and I handle this.

She smiles.
Besides, it sounds
like it's a
special day.

REPAIR

The first thing
Aiden says
when he walks
through the
front door:

I like your house.

I can't help
but snort.
Don't worry.
You don't have to
be nice about it.

He puts his hand
on the wall,
runs his fingers
across the
flaked paint.

I mean, it could
use some work,
he says.

But I could
help you repaint,
if you'd like.

And I know
Rosa's dad is
a plumber,

if you have
issues with
the pipes.

I reach for
his hand.

Really?
You mean it?
I ask.

It might not
be enough
to save
our house,
but it gives
me hope.

I'm not ready
to let it go.

Not without
one last
fight.

DINNER

We all sit
around the table:
Mom, Dad, Samantha,
Aiden, and me.

Aiden can't help
but ask for seconds.
This is so good,
he says between
forkfuls of brisket.

Mom offers to
pack up a serving
to take home,
for his mom.

When Aiden
gets up to go
to the bathroom,
Samantha says
we look so cute.

And I bet my face
turns brighter than
the carrots on
my plate.

THE END

Aiden and I
sneak downstairs
to find the perfect
movie to watch.

We curl up
on the couch,
flipping through
TV channels.

After all these weeks
in film club, this is
the first time we're
watching together.

What's your favorite
part of a movie?
I ask as I press
against his arm.

He leans back
and thinks for
a moment.

The ending is the
best part, for sure.

I shake my head.
Nah, no way.
Endings make me sad.

188

When the screen
fades to black,
the escape is over.

*A good ending isn't
really an ending,*
he says.
*It's just the end of
that part of the story.*

*Things keep
moving forward,
but they feel
different. Better.*

He slides his
fingers through mine.

His knuckles
are smooth to
the touch.

The bruises
are just about gone.

*That's the best—
an ending that
makes all the anger
and disappointment*

feel worth it.

FADE OUT:

to

the messy,
angry,
beautiful
real world.

WANT TO KEEP READING?

If you liked this book, check out another
book from West 44 Books:

CATCH ME IF I FALL
BY CLAUDIA RECINOS SELDEEN

ISBN: 9781978596351

BALANCING ACT

Hang
on
tight!

When I'm on a trapeze,
I defy gravity.

I'm a leaf
caught in a summer storm.
Twisting.
Spinning.

But there's always that voice
in the back of my mind,
whispering:

Hang
on
tight.

Don't
let
go.

Falling is not an option.

DANCE TRAPEZE

When I tell people
I'm a
trapeze artist,
their eyes
light up
like stars.

I know
they're thinking about
flying
       trapeze.
About acrobats
w h i z z i n g
through the air.

But
dance
       trapeze
is
different.

There's no
swinging.
No catching.
No letting go.

A
dance
       trapeze
doesn't
tick tock
back and forth.

A
dance
       trapeze
spins
in tight circles.

It twirls
and turns.

If you don't hold on,
it will
spin
you
right
off.

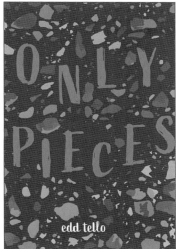

CHECK OUT MORE BOOKS AT:
www.west44books.com

An imprint of Enslow Publishing

WEST **44** BOOKS™

About the Author

Mel Mallory (she/her) works at a peer-led mental health organization. As a kid, she spent way too much time debating which VHS tape to rent at her local video store. She now lives in Maryland with her two guinea pigs. Her other verse novel, *Survive and Keep Surviving*, is about healing after experiencing mental distress and trauma. You can find her at melmallory.com.